Bob the Builder

Bob's Birthday

One morning, Wendy gathered the machines together in Bob's yard.

"Listen, everybody," she said. "It's Bob's birthday today and I've had a brilliant idea! Let's pretend it's just an ordinary day – and surprise Bob with a party tonight!"

"You mean, pretend it *isn't* Bob's birthday?" rumbled Roley.

"Won't Bob be disappointed if we don't wish him happy birthday?" asked Muck.

"We can wish him happy birthday later – at the party," Wendy explained. "But remember, it's a secret. Not a word to Bob!"

In the office, Bob was chatting to Pilchard.
"It's my birthday today," he said, excitedly.
"Prrrrr…." miaowed Pilchard, happily.
"I'd better get a move on," said Bob. "I expect everyone's waiting for me in the yard." He hurried outside.
"Here comes Bob," whispered Wendy, as Bob crossed the yard.
"'Morning, Wendy," he called cheerily.
"'Morning, Bob," Wendy replied.
"Hi, Bob!" chorused the machines.

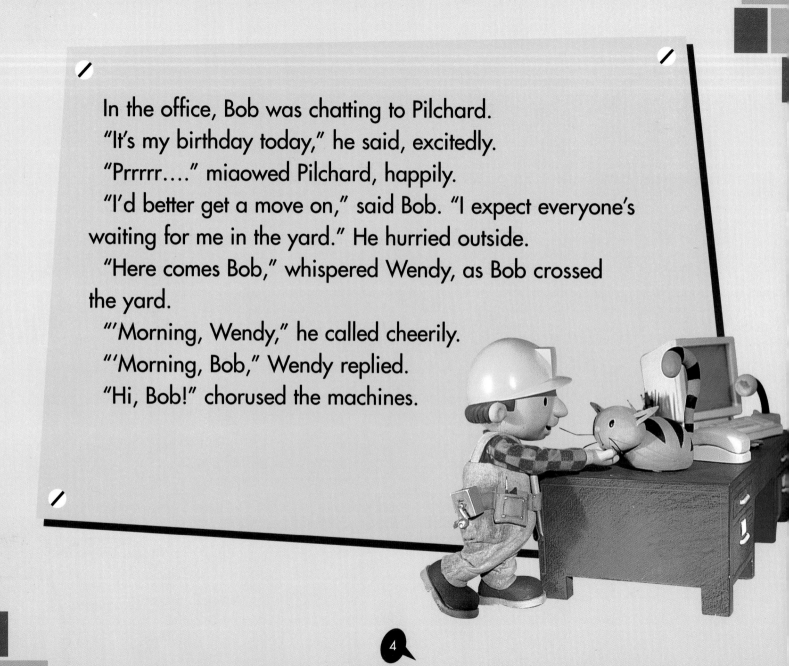

"Er… was there any post for me, Wendy?" asked Bob, with a hopeful smile.

"I don't think it's come yet," Wendy replied. "Were you expecting anything special?"

"Er, no. Nothing special," Bob replied, quickly.

"Isn't it time you were off to fix Farmer Pickles' stable wall?" said Wendy, briskly.

"Yes, there's plenty to do," Bob said. "Now let's see. I'll need Scoop to clear the site and Lofty to lift the planks of wood."

"That's good," rumbled Roley. "The rest of us can stay here and get ready for the – "

"Shhh, Roley!" dithered Lofty.

"Get ready for what?" asked Bob curiously, when Roley suddenly fell quiet.

"For…for…" gulped Roley.

"For LUNCH!" cried Wendy.

Bob shook his head. "Oh, well," he said, as he climbed aboard Scoop. "I'll be off then."

"'Bye, Bob. Have a nice day," Wendy said.

"I'll try," he mumbled glumly. "Bye…"

As Bob, Scoop and Lofty roared out of the yard, Wendy heaved a huge sigh of relief.

"Good! Now I can get on with baking Bob's birthday cake!"

When Bob, Scoop and Lofty got to Farmer Pickles' stable, Travis and Spud were there.

"Need any help?" asked Travis.

"No, thank you. I think we can manage," Bob replied as he examined the old planking.

E - e - e - e - k - k screeched the nails as he tugged hard.

"Pull harder, Bob!" yelled Spud.

"I'm doing my best," grunted Bob.

Suddenly the plank came loose and Bob fell over, flat onto his bottom!

"That was a tough one," he spluttered.

Spud roared with laughter.

"Ha-ha-ha-ha-ha!" he giggled.

"Can Bob fix it? Ha ha ha ha!"
Bob looked at Spud crossly.
Scoop roared forward to pick up the fallen plank.
"Move out of the way, Spud!" he chugged. "Some of us have got work to do."

Back at the yard, Dizzy and Muck watched Wendy make Bob's birthday cake.

"Cake making looks easy to me," said Muck. "You just throw everything together and mix it up."

"Just like making concrete!" giggled Dizzy.

"Bob loves your concrete, Dizzy," cried Muck. "Why don't we make him a concrete cake he can keep forever?"

"Yes!" Dizzy squeaked.

"Can we make it?" chanted Muck.

"Yes, we can!" laughed Dizzy.

Dizzy quickly whipped up a load of her very best concrete.
"OK, let's get it into the mould," she instructed.
"Mould...? What mould?" puzzled Muck.
"I can't just pour a load of concrete out onto the ground,"
Dizzy explained. "It'll run all over the yard and set like a big,
flat pancake."
"Wait there... I'll go and find something," said Muck.
A few minutes later, Muck trundled back with a big tyre
in his front shovel.
"Here it comes!" cried Dizzy.
The concrete plopped and glugged
into the tyre. "Perfect!" beamed Dizzy.

At Farmer Pickles' stable, Bob watched as Lofty slowly and carefully lowered a dangling plank.

"To me!" giggled Travis.

"To you, to me! He he he!" chuckled Spud.

Their teasing sent Lofty into one of his nervous jitters.

"Oooh!" he dithered.

"Aren't you two supposed to be delivering Farmer Pickles' eggs?" said Bob crossly.

"Right then!" said Travis, huffily starting up his engine. "We'll be off. Come on, Spud," he called sharply.

Off they went.

Back at the yard, Roley wasn't very impressed with Dizzy's concrete cake.

"It needs something to brighten it up," he said.

Muck and Dizzy stared at the concrete.

"I like it just the way it is," said Dizzy.

"Maybe Roley's right," said Muck. "Let's go and see what we can find."

Five minutes later, Dizzy and Muck came clanking back.

"Aren't they pretty?" cried Dizzy, as she showered feathers onto the cake.

"Look what I found!" said Muck, scooping up a load of coloured leaves.

Roley smiled. "That's brightened it up all right," he rumbled.

Dizzy, Muck and Roley were so busy admiring the cake that they didn't see Spud and Travis drive up to Bob's house with their egg delivery.

"M...m...mmm!" said Spud, drooling at the sight of the delicious birthday cake on the kitchen table. He scooped some icing onto his finger – and popped it into his mouth!

"Spud! Fingers off!" yelled Wendy, walking into the kitchen. "That's Bob's birthday cake!"

"I'm sorry, Wendy," Spud mumbled, looking ashamed of himself. "It looked so good and I'm so hungry!"

"I was about to put the candles on," said Wendy.

"Can I help?" asked Spud. "Please?"

"Well..." frowned Wendy. "Well, all right then."

"Spud's on the job!" laughed the scarecrow.

As Bob nailed the last plank into Farmer Pickles' stable wall, his mobile phone rang out.

"Perhaps this is a birthday phone call," he said, hopefully.

"Hi, Bob," Wendy answered. "I just wondered when you'd be getting back."

"We've just finished," Bob told her. "So we'll be back quite soon. Why... any special reason?"

"No, no," Wendy replied, breezily. "I've just got a few letters for you to sign. 'Bye!"

Bob sighed heavily as he switched off his phone.

"No Happy Birthday Bob, then," he murmured.

Scoop winked at Lofty. "Come on, Bob," he called. "Home time!"

Wendy, Muck, Dizzy and Roley had decorated a table and covered it with cakes and presents.

"It looks beautiful!" said Wendy, as the guests waited for Bob in the yard.

"Oooh!" squealed Dizzy. "I can hear Scoop. He's coming!"

Bob couldn't believe his eyes when he arrived back at the yard and everybody burst out singing.

"Bob the Builder,
      it's his birthday!
Bob the Builder,
      yes, it is!
It's Bob's birthday,
      can we sing it?
It's Bob's birthday –
      yes, we can!"

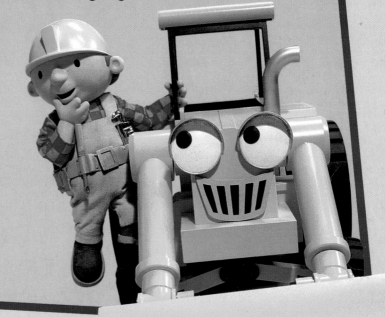

"Surprise! Surprise!" laughed Wendy. "Happy Birthday, Bob!"

Grinning with delight, Bob leapt off Scoop.

"And I thought you'd all forgotten my birthday," he chuckled.

"Forget your birthday, Bob?" teased Wendy. "Never!"

"**Look**, Bob!" roared Muck. "You've got **two** cakes."

Bob stared at his two beautiful cakes.

"A real cake to eat and a concrete cake I can keep forever!" he said, happily. "Oh, thank you for a lovely surprise party."

"Just one more thing," said Wendy as she handed Bob a big pile of birthday cards. "Your post!"

"All for me?" gasped Bob.

"Of course," laughed Wendy. "You're the Birthday Builder!"

"Hurray!" everybody cheered.

"Now please, please, may I have a slice of that yummy cake?" begged Spud.

"Of course you may," said Bob, as he cut his birthday cake and gave Spud a huge piece. "Here you are, Spud!"

Spud stuffed the cake into his mouth.

"Spud's on the job, Bob. Ha-ha-ha!"

THE END!